CONTEMPORARY'S
LET'S READ TOGETHER
What Will School Be Like?

Clairece Feagin

Project Editor
Sarah Conroy

Consultants and Field-testers
The Students and Staff
at the
Adult Learning Source
Family Literacy Program
Denver, CO

Pamela M. Smith
Program Coordinator

Sandra J. Dawson

Pamela K. Harris

Camilla M. Martinez

CB
CONTEMPORARY
BOOKS
CHICAGO

Published by Contemporary Books, Inc.
180 North Michigan Avenue, Chicago, Illinois 60601
Manufactured in the United States of America
International Standard Book Number: 0-8092-4013-0

Published simultaneously in Canada by
Fitzhenry & Whiteside
195 Allstate Parkway
Valleywood Business Park
Markham, Ontario L3R 4T8
Canada

Editorial Director
Caren Van Slyke

Editorial
Cathy Hobbins
Erica Pochis
Chris Benton
Cyndy Raucci
Ilene Weismehl

Editorial Production Manager
Norma Fioretti

Production Editor
Marina Micari

Cover Design
Lois Stein

Cover Illustrator
Quang Ho

Cover Inset Illustrator
Kathy Petrauskas

Interior Illustrator
Linda Reilly

Art & Production
Jan Geist

CHILD'S STORY

Contents

Characters

James Willis, age 6

Dion, James's cousin, age 12

Mrs. Willis

Mr. Willis

Mr. Hall, the school secretary

Miss Cruz, the first-grade teacher

> Turn the book over to read a story
> just for parents.

How do you feel about going to school?

Chapter 1   What's School Like?

Six-year-old James Willis sat on the front steps of his apartment building. He watched a row of tiny ants crawl across the sidewalk. On hot days like today, the steps were his favorite place. It was too hot to run or play ball or even ride a bike.

James put his finger on the ground for the ants to crawl over. He had a lot on his mind today. The summer was almost over, and tomorrow he would enroll in first grade.

What will first grade be like? James wondered. What will I do in school? Will I have a nice teacher? Will the other kids like me?

James heard the sound of a radio getting louder. He heard the front door of the building open. Without even looking up, he knew it was his cousin Dion coming through the door.

Dion was 12. He lived one floor above James. James was glad to see Dion. He liked to listen to Dion's radio and hear him talk about things the big kids did.

Last year, Dion rode a big school bus every day. Sometimes James used to walk Dion to the bus stop. James thought it would be fun to ride the school bus.

"What's school like?" James asked Dion. "Is it fun?"

"Fun? No way!" Dion said. "The only fun part about school is recess."

James hoped Dion didn't mean it. James didn't know much about first grade, but he knew that he would learn to read there. Reading was going to be fun.

"Did you bring any comic books?" James asked Dion. James liked to look at the pictures and make up stories.

"No," Dion told him.

Dion sat down on the steps and put his radio beside him. The two boys listened to the music in silence. It was too hot even to talk.

How did James feel about first grade before he went to enroll?

Chapter 2 A Look at the School

James's mother stayed home from her job the next morning to take him to enroll in school. As they walked up to the school, they saw groups of older children talking outside the school building.

Look how big the school is, James thought. He held his mother's hand tightly as they walked down a long hall. The walls were decorated with bright pictures. There were colorful signs, too. James wondered what they said.

"Where do I enroll a child for first grade?" Mrs. Willis asked a man at a table in the hall.

"Right here," the man said, smiling at them.

"What's your name?" he asked James.

"James Willis," James said softly.

The man gave Mrs. Willis some papers to fill out.

"Are you the teacher?" James asked.

"No. I'm the secretary. My name is Mr. Hall. Your teacher is in her classroom."

"What's her name?" James asked.

"Your teacher will be Miss Cruz."

"Is she nice?" James asked.

"I think she's very nice," Mr. Hall told him. "But why don't you go see for yourself? As soon as we get you enrolled, you can go meet Miss Cruz and see your room."

"Is that the first-grade room?" James asked, pointing to the classroom nearest the table.

"No," Mr. Hall answered. "The first-grade room is at the end of this hall."

James wanted to run to the first-grade room right that minute. Then he felt his mother's hand on his shoulder. How did she always know what he was thinking?

Mrs. Willis finished filling out the papers and gave them to Mr. Hall.

"Which room is it?" she asked, taking James's hand in hers.

"It's at the end of the hall on the right. There's a sign on the door saying First Grade."

Chapter 3   Meeting the Teacher

James walked as fast as he could, tugging at his mother's hand to make her walk faster. He hoped the teacher would be nice. He hoped the other children would like him. James felt very happy that he was going to go to school.

A friendly woman greeted James when he walked into the first-grade room.

"Hello," she said. "I'm Miss Cruz. This is the first-grade room. Are you a first grader?"

"Yes," James answered, looking at all the desks in the big room.

"What's your name?" Miss Cruz asked.

"James Willis," he said. "Do kids sit here?" he asked, pointing to the desks.

"Yes. Every child has a desk. Would you like to find your desk?" Miss Cruz asked. Then she led James to a desk near the middle of the room.

"This will be your desk," she told him. "When you come to school next Monday, this is where you will sit. Here is the place for your books. And if you bring your lunch, you can put your lunch box here," she added, showing him the special shelf for lunch boxes. "These hooks on the wall are for coats when the weather gets colder.

"Be sure his name is on his lunch box," Miss Cruz told Mrs. Willis. "It's easy for the lunch boxes to get mixed up."

"This is a big room!" James said.

"I hope it will be a happy room for you, James," Miss Cruz said.

Just then two more children and their parents came into the room.

"We're looking for Miss Cruz," they said.

"I'm Miss Cruz," the teacher told them.

James looked at the other children. He had never seen them before. Then he looked at all the desks in this big room. Would there be this many children in first grade? What if he didn't know any of the other children in his class? What if someone else got his lunch box?

"We'd better go home now," Mrs. Willis told James. "I've got to get to work by 11 o'clock."

"Good-bye," Miss Cruz called. "See you Monday morning, James."

If you go to school, how did you feel the first time you saw your classroom? Draw a picture of your classroom.

Chapter 4   Riding the Bus

On the first day of school, James got up extra early. He washed his face and put on his best shirt. He looked forward to school, but he was also a little bit scared.

James put his new pencil in his pocket and picked up the lunch his mother had made for him. Then he walked to the bus stop with Dion.

The school bus was very crowded. James wanted to hold Dion's hand so he wouldn't get lost, but Dion wouldn't let him.

"You're too big to hold anyone's hand," Dion told him. Then Dion moved through the crowd of children to the back of the bus to talk with the other big kids.

James sat down and looked around him. He saw a few kids he knew, but they were older than he was. They all were talking with their friends and didn't notice him. James felt very small and alone. He looked out the window to see what places the bus passed.

When James got off the bus, he saw his teacher, Miss Cruz, standing in front of the school. Some parents were standing with their children, talking to Miss Cruz. James wished his mother and dad had come with him. But his parents both left for work before it was time for him to go to the bus stop.

James followed Miss Cruz and the other children into the first-grade room. Miss Cruz showed the children to their desks, and James sat down.

Chapter 5   **Welcome to First Grade**

"Good morning, children," Miss Cruz said after the children were all seated. "Welcome to first grade. I bet you wonder what we're going to do at school.

"One thing we'll do is learn about numbers," she said. Miss Cruz held up some large cards with numbers drawn on them.

"How many of you can count to 10?" she asked.

Lots of hands shot up.

I know the numbers, James thought. I can count to 10. So he put his hand up, too.

"Great!" Miss Cruz said. "Then let's all count to 10."

"One, two, three," the children began to count together.

James didn't say anything at first. When the children got to *four*, James began to say the numbers with the other children. He spoke very softly. If he said one wrong, he wanted to be sure no one heard.

"We'll also learn about the letters," Miss Cruz

said. She pointed to some very big letters on the wall above the chalkboard.

"Soon we'll start working on our reading skills," she added.

James felt good when he heard Miss Cruz say "reading skills." He was excited about reading!

Miss Cruz showed the children the other parts of the room. There was a place to paint and a place to wash up. There were shelves of books and a big table full of puzzles. On one table sat a big wire cage.

"This cage is for our pet," Miss Cruz told the children. "Next week we'll get a rabbit. We'll all take turns feeding the rabbit. You can even help me clean out his cage."

James didn't have a pet of his own. A rabbit in the classroom would be great. He could hardly wait.

If you go to school, what is your favorite thing to do there?

Chapter 6 Homework

James liked first grade. He liked learning new things. He liked to paint and do puzzles. He was glad to have new friends and liked playing with the other children outside. And he really liked to help take care of the pet rabbit, Snowy.

Every day Miss Cruz gave the children new things to do in class. Some days they practiced writing numbers and letters. Some days they drew pictures and told stories. Every day the teacher read to the class. James thought first grade was going fine.

Then one day, Miss Cruz told the children that they were ready to start doing homework. James wasn't sure he would like this. He had heard Dion talk about homework, and Dion certainly didn't like it.

"Why do we have to do homework?" one of the children asked.

"Homework will help you think about the things you learn in class," Miss Cruz told them. "It will help you learn new things."

Miss Cruz showed the children their homework page. It looked like the pages they sometimes did in class. James decided this homework wouldn't be too bad.

"You'll have a little bit of homework every week," Miss Cruz said. "Your homework should take about 10 or 15 minutes. You'll need a quiet place at home to work on it — somewhere away from the TV.

"When you bring your homework back to school the next day, you can put it in this basket on my desk. I'll look at your papers to see if you understand the work. If you have trouble, I'll know what to help you with," she said.

"And on Fridays, you can take your papers home to show your parents."

How do you feel about homework?

When James got home after school, he saw that the homework wasn't hard. He finished the page and put it on the table by his bed.

Chapter 7   **Nobody's Perfect**

The next morning, Miss Cruz greeted each child at the classroom door. She had the homework basket in her hands. James saw other children putting their homework in the basket as they entered the room.

Oh, no, James thought. My homework paper!

It's still on my table at home! He wanted to turn around and leave, but Miss Cruz had already seen him.

"I put mine by my bed yesterday. I guess it's still there," he told her.

"You can bring it tomorrow," she said with a smile. "You'll have another homework page tonight. Maybe you can ask your mom and dad to remind you so you won't forget it," she said.

The next morning, James didn't have his homework again.

"I . . . I forgot to do it," he told Miss Cruz, looking down at his feet.

"James, that's OK," Miss Cruz said. "I understand. But you should set aside a special time each day for homework. Right after supper is good for some children. Others like to do their homework just before supper.

"You can bring both pages tomorrow," she added. "Ask your parents to help you remember. If you have trouble doing your homework, maybe they can help you."

What kinds of things do your parents help you with?

That night James remembered about his homework. But his parents were watching TV, and there wasn't a quiet place for him to sit down. James didn't know what to do. He put the papers by his bed and went to watch TV.

The next day, James didn't want to go to school. He hadn't even started his homework. He thought Miss Cruz would be mad at him.

"I don't feel good today," he told his mother when he went to the kitchen to eat.

"What's the matter?" Mrs. Willis asked, putting her hand on his forehead. "You don't have a fever. I think you'd better go to school. If you get sick, you can go to the nurse."

Why didn't James want to go to school? Do you think he should talk to his parents about it?

Chapter 8   The Note

That afternoon, Miss Cruz called James to her desk as he was going to the bus. She handed him a folded piece of paper.

"James, I'd like you to take this note home to your mom and dad," she told him.

"Note?" James wasn't sure what to say. "Am I . . . ," he started. "Are you . . ."

"It's OK, James. You're not in trouble. I just want to talk to your parents. They can help you with your homework. And they can help you remember to bring it back to school," Miss Cruz said.

James gave the note to his dad after supper.

"Is anything wrong at school?" his dad asked.

"Miss Cruz says I'm not in trouble!" James said. He ran outside to play.

At bedtime, Mrs. Willis tucked James in.

"Is anything wrong at school?" she asked. "Miss Cruz asked your dad and me to come to talk with her tomorrow. Do you know what it's about?"

"She says I need your help," James said, looking away.

"Well, that doesn't sound too bad! We love to help our little boy. I'm sure things will be OK," Mrs. Willis said, giving James a good-night hug.

Chapter 9   Working Together

The next day, James worried about the meeting with Miss Cruz.

What if I'm not smart enough for school? he wondered. What if Mom and Dad won't help?

When his parents got home, James ran to meet them. His dad gave him a big hug and carried him to the couch.

"Miss Cruz told us a lot of good things about you," Mrs. Willis began. "She told us how you named Snowy and how much fun it is having you in her class. She said you have a lot of friends at school, too."

"But I forget to do my homework," James cried.

"We can help you with that, son," Mr. Willis said. "You can work at the kitchen table. And we'll turn off the TV while you're doing your homework.

"You can ask for help if you need it," he added. "You can show me what you're learning. I'd like that."

"Are you mad at me?" James asked.

"Of course not, son," said Mrs. Willis. "And Miss Cruz isn't mad at you. We just want you to do your best, and Miss Cruz showed us ways to help you."

"Am I smart enough for school?" James cried.

"Oh, yes! Miss Cruz said you were a very smart boy," Mr. Willis said proudly. "Everyone needs help sometimes. You just need to ask."

"We can sit with you when you do your homework," said Mrs. Willis. "We'll all learn something!"

Think about the Story

1. James was excited about learning to read. What are you most excited to learn?

2. Before he enrolled in first grade, James was a little bit worried about school. Have you ever worried about school?

   What made you feel better?

3. Do you think that you will do better in school if you ask your parents for help? Why?

Ideas from the Story

Most children are excited about going to school. They want to learn to read and do artwork and learn about animals. They want to learn math and to write stories.

Sometimes children make mistakes and are afraid they'll get in trouble. If this happens, then school can be a frightening place.

Children can feel better about school if they talk about their fears. They can talk to their teacher, and they can talk to their parents. They can show their parents what they do in school. And children can always ask for help. Talking about school can help make school fun.

End of Child's Story

Turn the book over to read a story
just for parents.

PARENT'S STORY

Contents

Characters

Frank Willis
Pat Willis
James Willis, age 6
Miss Cruz, James's teacher

Turn the book over to read a story
for parents and children.

What are some things parents can do to help their children do well in school?

Chapter 1   **Enrolling in School**

"It's hard to believe James is starting first grade already," Frank Willis said.

"Yes. It seems like only yesterday he was learning to walk and talk," Pat Willis agreed. "I think he's excited about school," she added. "He's been talking about it a lot."

"I hope he gets a good teacher," Frank said. "I never liked school much myself. Maybe it was because I never did very well in school. I've always wished I'd learned to read better."

"I just hope he doesn't get in with a bad bunch of kids," Pat said.

"Me too," Frank agreed. "We'll just have to keep an eye on him. He enrolls tomorrow, right?" he asked.

"Yes," his wife said. "I went by the doctor's office and got a record of all his shots today. The school has to see those before he can enroll."

"I'd like to take him to enroll," Frank said. "But we're pouring cement on a new job in the morning, so I can't take off."

"It's OK. I'm taking off work in the morning.

I told my boss I'd be in by 11," Pat said. "I thought about getting my sister, Denise, to take James, but I think it's important to see the school for myself. And I want to meet his teacher. I'm glad my boss was understanding about it," she added.

"I'd like to go and see the school, too," Frank said.

"Maybe they'll let you visit the school some other time," Pat said.

Pat was a little bit nervous as she and James walked toward the school building the next morning. It had been years since she was in school. And the school looked very large.

How many children go to this school? she wondered. She hoped they had enough teachers to teach so many children — and to watch them so they didn't get into trouble.

And what if James got lost in such a big building? She hoped the first-grade room was easy to find.

There were quite a lot of people at the school. Older children were outside talking. Younger children were inside with their parents.

Pat could tell that James was a little bit frightened, because he held her hand so tightly. She wasn't sure where she and James should go. Then she saw a man sitting behind a table down the hall.

"Where do I enroll a child for first grade?" she asked him.

Pat was relieved to learn she was in the right place. The man was very helpful. He talked to James while Pat filled out the papers to enroll James.

Thank goodness I remembered to bring all these forms, she thought. She unfolded James's birth certificate. Then she took the doctor's records to copy down the immunizations James had been given.

Meeting the Teacher

When Pat finished all the papers, she and James walked down the hall to the first-grade room. She was as eager as James to see his room and meet his teacher. Denise's son, Dion, had never done well in school. He didn't like to go to school, and he never learned to read like he should. Pat wanted to make sure the same thing didn't happen to James.

She was happy to see how kind Miss Cruz was. James seemed to like Miss Cruz right away. That pleased Pat. Both she and her husband wanted James to do well in school.

Pat wanted to stay and talk with Miss Cruz a while, but other parents arrived with their children. Besides, Pat had to go to work. She promised herself that she'd come back some other time and talk with Miss Cruz.

> What information did Pat need to bring to enroll James in school? Why did she want to meet the teacher?

That night, Frank was eager to hear all about James's school. He listened carefully to all Pat told him about it.

"Did James seem to like his teacher?" Frank asked.

"Oh, yes," Pat told him. "She is very friendly and seems to care a lot about the children. James felt right at home in her classroom."

"That's good. I don't want him to hate school like Dion does."

Chapter 2   Does James Have a Problem?

Things went well for James for several weeks. Frank and Pat were glad to see him enjoying school and learning new things.

Then one morning James seemed upset. He told Pat he didn't feel well. He wanted to stay home from school. She could tell that he didn't have a fever or a cold. She wondered if something was wrong at school.

That night, she and her husband were in the kitchen before supper.

"I'm worried about James," Pat said. "He wanted to stay home from school today, but he wasn't really sick."

"I thought things were going so well for him at school," Frank said.

"If this keeps up, maybe I'll call his teacher," Pat said. "I talked with Denise about James. She said to call the school. She said if anything's going wrong there, we'd better take care of it now, before things get worse."

"Can parents just call the school anytime?" Frank asked.

"Denise said it is our right as parents to find out everything that's going on with James at school. She said if she'd done that, maybe Dion wouldn't have the problems he has now."

"Well, if James keeps acting this way, and if he won't tell us what's wrong, I guess I could call the teacher. I could just ask if James is having any problems," Frank said. But he was not comfortable with the idea of calling a teacher he'd never met.

"Maybe you should call her because you're the one who met her," he told his wife.

"If James keeps trying to avoid school, I will," she agreed.

If you were Pat or Frank, what would you do?

The Note

During supper, James seemed sad. When his parents asked him about school, he said it was OK.

Right after supper, James handed his dad a note from Miss Cruz.

"Miss Cruz says I'm not in trouble!" James said to his dad. James ran outside to play.

Frank took the note, but he didn't think he could read it. He gave it to his wife.

"What's it say?" he asked.

Pat was almost afraid to read the note. Was James in some sort of trouble at school? Was he keeping up with his work? Was he learning what he was supposed to learn?

Then she read it out loud:

Dear Mr. and Mrs. Willis,

Could you come in one afternoon this week? I'd like to talk with you about James.

Sincerely,
Miss Cruz

"She's written her home phone number here," Pat added. "I guess it's OK to call her now."

"I guess we'd better," Frank agreed. "I can get off early tomorrow afternoon if she can meet with us then."

Chapter 3   Meeting with Miss Cruz

Frank felt very nervous as they walked into the classroom. He stayed a few steps behind his wife, wishing he'd let her come to see Miss Cruz alone. As he looked around the room, he wondered which desk was James's.

"Hello." Miss Cruz smiled. "I'm glad you could come in. I'm glad to meet you, Mr. Willis. Why don't I show you around the room? Then we can sit and talk about James's work.

"I really like having James in my class," Miss Cruz said. "He's such a happy child. He gets along well with the other children."

Pat looked at her husband and smiled. It made both of them feel good to hear such nice things about James.

"He's very helpful taking care of Snowy, our pet rabbit," Miss Cruz added. "Did you know that James is the one who named Snowy?" she asked.

"He really likes that rabbit," Frank said, feeling a little more relaxed. "He talks about Snowy all the time."

"It makes us feel good to hear that James is getting along so well in your class," Pat said.

"We thought he must be in some trouble when you asked us to come here," Frank said.

"Oh, no," Miss Cruz told them. "James isn't in any trouble. He's very well behaved in class. But I do want to talk with you about his schoolwork.

"James is quick to understand the things we learn in class," she continued. "But I want to make sure he keeps up with the class. I think that if we all work together, we can help James do very well in school."

"Is James falling behind in his work?" Pat asked.

"No, not yet. But I'm giving the children some homework now, to help them remember what they've learned. So far, James hasn't brought his homework back to school."

"What homework?" Frank asked. "We haven't seen any."

"Well, I've only sent two pages home so far," Miss Cruz said. "So James isn't really behind. I like to tell all the parents about the homework I'm giving the children. That way, parents will know about the homework. They can help their children learn."

"What kind of homework do you give?" asked Pat.

"All different kinds. Sometimes I have them draw a picture so they can tell a story about it the next day. Sometimes I give them a page to practice their numbers or letters on. And

sometimes I give them projects, like finding certain leaves or special things to touch.

"We use homework in different ways," Miss Cruz continued. "Usually, homework is fun for children. When I look at children's homework, I can tell whether they understand the work. I can tell where each child is having trouble, so I can help them understand the material."

"How often do you give the children homework?" Pat asked.

"Usually two days a week," Miss Cruz said. "Some weeks may have less than others."

"And James didn't do his homework this week?" Frank asked.

"He didn't bring it back to school. He probably just forgot," said Miss Cruz.

Pat looked at her husband. "No wonder James didn't want to go to school yesterday," she said. "He must have thought he'd get in trouble."

"Oh, no," Miss Cruz laughed. "First graders aren't expected to be perfect! What's important is that we get James started on the right track."

Have your children ever wanted to stay home from school when they weren't sick? What did you do to help them?

Tips from Miss Cruz

"Is there anything we can do to help James?" Frank asked. "We want him to do well in school. I never . . . well, I didn't learn to read very well when I was in school. And James's cousin is starting off like I did. We don't want that to happen to James."

Miss Cruz thought for a moment. "James has made good progress. I don't think you have to worry about him. But there are things you can do. He needs a quiet place where he can do his homework, away from the TV. It's best if he can do it in the same place and at the same time every night. That will help him learn good study habits," Miss Cruz explained.

"You may have to remind him to bring his homework to school until he gets into the habit," she added.

"We want to help James any way we can," Pat said.

13

"You can talk to James about what he's learning. Ask him questions. And if he asks you questions, try to explain the answer to him," said Miss Cruz. "It will also help James if you read to him every day.

"Mr. Willis, you said you didn't learn to read very well," Miss Cruz said. "I know of several different classes for adults who want to work on reading skills. Classes meet day or night, and some meet on weekends. If you want to improve your reading, I can recommend some classes to you.

"You know," she continued, "if James sees both of you reading, he will be more likely to read at home himself. This will help him in school."

"I don't know," Frank said, looking at his wife. "I work all day. Besides, I'm kind of old to go back to school."

"I understand," Miss Cruz said. "But these classes are for adults only, and there are many people who go to them. Many classes are free. Here's a list of phone numbers. Think about it. If you decide you'd like to go, call these programs. They'll tell you when and where classes meet."

"I'll think about it," Frank said, taking the list. "If it will help James, it would be worth it."

"We're glad you asked us to come in," Pat said. "We'll be sure to try all we can to help James do well."

"Thanks for coming," Miss Cruz said. "I'll keep in touch. I'm sure that by working together we can help James do his best in school.

"We all want the same thing for James," she added. "We want him to be happy and to learn. Children get along better in school when the parents and the teacher work together as a team. If you have any questions or see James having any problems, you can always call me or come in to talk. If I can't come to the phone when you call, just leave a message in the school office. Then I'll call you later.

"I hope you can both come to Parents' Night at school," Miss Cruz told them. "It will be a time for parents to learn more about the school. We'll talk about questions the parents have, and you can also meet parents of other students."

"Thanks. We'd like to come," Frank said as he and his wife got up to leave.

What do you think made Frank decide to call some adult reading programs?

Chapter 4   Reading Together

Soon James and his parents got into a routine. On homework days, James showed his work to his parents. Frank asked James to explain what it was about. He watched James do the work.

On Saturday mornings, Frank went to a reading class for adults. He was surprised to find so many people in the class. There were two people in the class that Frank already knew.

Frank's reading class had homework, too. On some evenings, he and James did their homework together.

One night after James had finished his homework, Frank picked up a book and began to read a story. James looked at his dad. Then he looked at his mother. Then he climbed onto his dad's lap and laid his head on his dad's chest.

"That's my favorite story," James said when his dad finished reading.

"Mine too, pal," Frank said. "Mine too."

Think about the Story

1. When a child first goes to school, parents can worry about many different things. What are some things that you might worry about?

   What could you do to ease your worries?

2. Pat and Frank's nephew, Dion, has not learned to read as well as he should. What can Dion's mother do to help him improve his reading skills?

   What would you do if Dion were your son?

3. How do you feel about Frank's decision to go to an adult reading class?

Ideas from the Story

It is every parent's right to know what goes on in his or her child's school. No matter what question a parent has, it is OK to call the school and ask for a meeting with the child's teacher.

Children get along much better in school when parents and teachers work as a team. Parents should make sure they meet their child's teacher each year and talk with the teacher when their child has a problem.

Parents' Nights are good times to learn about your children's school. Getting involved with the school shows children that you care about how they are doing in school. Knowing that you care can help your children want to do their best.

To help their children, parents can:
- talk to their children about school
- read to their children
- help their children with homework

Parents who haven't yet learned to read can go to class part-time, day or night. Adult reading classes are held in libraries and high schools in most cities. Most of these classes are free of charge.

End of Parent's Story